Hunter's Moon

BY JOHN TOWNSEND

ILLUSTRATED BY SEAN DIETRICH

Librarian Reviewer
Marci Peschke
Librarian, Dallas Independent School District
MA Education Reading Specialist, Stephen F. Austin State University
Learning Resources Endorsement, Texas Women's University

Reading Consultant
Elizabeth Stedem
Educator/Consultant, Colorado Springs, CO
MA in Elementary Education, University of Denver, CO

STONE ARCH BOOKS
Minneapolis   San Diego

First published in the United States in 2007
by Stone Arch Books,
151 Good Counsel Drive, P.O. Box 669,
Mankato, Minnesota 56002
www.stonearchbooks.com

First published by Evans Brothers Ltd,
2A Portman Mansions, Chiltern Street,
London W1U 6NR, United Kingdom

Copyright © 2003 Evans Brothers Ltd

Library of Congress Cataloging-in-Publication Data
Townsend, John, 1955–

    Hunter's Moon / by John Townsend; illustrated by Sean Dietrich.
    p. cm. — (Shade Books)
    Summary: As Halloween approaches, Neil has a growing fear of
the woods on the farm where he is filling in as gamekeeper since, besides
the rumor that a big cat is loose, he has also received a warning to
"beware the nights of the Hunter's Moon" which are about to begin.
    ISBN-13: 978-1-59889-352-6 (library binding)
    ISBN-10: 1-59889-352-1 (library binding)
    ISBN-13: 978-1-59889-447-9 (paperback)
    ISBN-10: 1-59889-447-1 (paperback)
    [1. Supernatural—Fiction. 2. Gamekeepers—Fiction. 3. Forests
and forestry—Fiction. 4. Panthers—Fiction.] I. Dietrich, Sean, ill.
II. Title.
PZ7.T66368Hun 2007
[Fic]—dc22   2006026876

Art Director: Heather Kindseth
Graphic Designer: Kay Fraser

1 2 3 4 5 6 12 11 10 09 08 07

Printed in the United States of America

TABLE OF CONTENTS

CHAPTER 1

EYES IN THE DARK

Neil was scared, but he didn't know why, not at first. The dark had never bothered him until now.

As the trees reached up around him and the wind stirred the bare twigs, he sensed something was there, something alive. It wasn't far away, and it was watching him.

The beam from his flashlight swept across the darkness and pointed into the woods. Deep blackness lurked at the edges of the trees and bushes.

He couldn't see anything, but he knew something was moving. Dead leaves crunched.

Something was there. An icy shiver ran down the back of Neil's neck.

He went back to the pile of wood and took a box of matches from his pocket.

He would feel safer once the bonfire was burning. A warm glow of orange light might melt the fear. The matchbox shook in his clumsy fingers.

As he bent down to strike a match, he heard scraping behind him.

The match snapped and the spark died.

His heart pounded and his throat felt dry. He reached for another match, anything to kill the thick darkness.

Neil felt silly.

He knew every inch of these woods. He'd lit bonfires after dark many times. It was his job to burn the dead wood.

He was used to being alone. That's what he liked about working outdoors. He loved the woods and being outside in all kinds of weather. He loved the quiet when no one was nearby.

But now he felt he wasn't alone.

A pair of eyes watched him. They flashed tiny sparks of light as flames from Neil's fire burned the dry twigs. The pile of branches was soon on fire. It hissed, crackled, and sparked in the darkness.

As the breeze fanned the flames, the whole pile was a blaze of dancing light. Smoke rolled up into orange branches and roosting birds.

Neil threw some dead leaves into the flames and watched them burn. He turned to peer into the woods just as the eyes hid behind a tree. Thick smoke swirled into the night and drifted across the moon.

An owl screeched above him and flapped away into the blackness. Neil turned suddenly, thinking that eyes were following his every move. He heard a deep growl just a few steps away. Neil spun around in the mud, stumbled, and ran.

The fire fizzed. It soon shrank to a small red pool of light before dying once and for all. Then someone's feet kicked embers into the damp grass. The same feet that prowled each night through silent woods, eyes watching, staring upward, always upward, to greet the Hunter's Moon.

9

CHAPTER 2

WORKING IN
THE WOODS

Neil had always wanted to work in the countryside. He helped his uncle most weekends at one of the farms nearby.

They paid him to help in the fields, but he had soon shown real skills for taking care of the young birds.

Neil had a sharp eye for any danger to the chicks. If a weasel or badger got through the fence, Neil was there like a shot. Nothing escaped his eyes and ears.

Jeff Barnard, one of Neil's uncle's friends, wanted to give Neil a job.

Jeff had inherited his family's farm, but it took a lot of money to run it. So Jeff opened his land to hunters and hikers and schools that needed field trips for students.

Jeff was one of those wise old country men who'd worked on the land his whole life. He was full of old sayings that made Neil laugh.

"See the water on the tip of that birch leaf? Tomorrow will be a fine day," Jeff might say.

But one morning, Jeff was reading the newspaper. "The bank over in Newport was robbed yesterday," Jeff said. He whistled. "They won't say how much the crooks got away with, but I'll bet it was a lot!"

"Says there's a reward for finding the money, too," Jeff added.

"Maybe the robbers will come through the woods," said Neil. "We could always use the cash."

"We don't need it that bad," said Jeff. "So were you thinking of taking the day off to go hunt for some bad guys?"

Neil laughed. "Fat chance with all those fence posts to put in. And look at that bright blue sky. A perfect day to work!"

Jeff shook his head. "Robin knows best. Look at that robin chirping on that log. That's a sure sign of rain."

By two o'clock a storm had already begun. Neil was amazed. Even though he knew a lot about nature, he still had plenty to learn from Jeff.

So Neil was upset when Jeff had to miss work because of an accident. Jeff had been building a footbridge over the stream when one of the supports had broken. He had crawled through the woods for hours before he got help.

While Jeff was away, Neil did all the jobs. He worked all hours, often after dark.

That's when he first felt uneasy. Autumn was always a busy time, with plenty of cutting and clearing to do.

"Clear and burn. Just keep clearing and burning," were Jeff's orders. But Neil wished that Jeff were there.

For the first time in his life, Neil began to feel frightened in the woods. What were those weird scratch marks at the base of an oak tree? Deep grooves, like claw marks. Why were there splashes of blood in one of the bird feeders?

There was something else, too: something behind the trees. Then there was a smell. It was near the broken footbridge where Jeff had fallen. Neil sensed fear here, fear of eyes somewhere in the shadows.

CHAPTER 3

TANYA

The girl walked like a ghost through the morning mist. She drifted along the footpath at the edge of the wood. The pale sunlight trickled through the trees and touched her face.

Neil looked up from raking leaves and was startled by her. The girl looked mysterious in a swirl of dappled light and October mist.

"Hi!" she called. For a moment, Neil was speechless.

"Lost your tongue?" the girl said. She smiled. Her dark eyes sparkled under a sweep of shining black hair.

Neil stared for a few seconds, first at her face, then slowly down to her muddy jeans and shoes.

She read his mind. "I slipped. It's very wet," she said.

"Are you lost?" he asked. It seemed like a dumb thing to say. He wished he hadn't. She certainly didn't seem lost.

"No. Not at all. Hey, I remember you." She smiled again.

What a nice smile, Neil thought. But who was she? He wouldn't have forgotten a face like hers. "Really?" he said, resting his elbow on the handle of the rake.

"Yeah. You were in the year below me at school. My friend liked you."

Neil felt himself blush. He still had no idea who she was.

"I'm Tanya," she said with a smile, reading his mind again. "Are there badgers around here?"

"Why do you ask?" Neil didn't mean to snap at her, but he was suddenly on his guard. People who asked about badgers were not to be trusted.

Some of the badger nests had been destroyed the month before. All the animals had been taken.

"My project." Tanya waved a pencil. Neil saw the sketch pad under her arm. "I'm an art student. I'm really into nature right now. I'd love to see a baby badger."

"You might see more than badgers," Neil said without thinking. The fears of his last few nights were getting to him.

Tanya moved closer and her dark eyes stared into his.

"Do you mean the beast? Everyone's talking about it at school. They say there's a panther on the loose somewhere around here. Dark and deadly, like me!" She made a playful snarl and clawed the air.

Neil had heard the rumors. They'd been going around for years.

But for the first time, he really felt like something was prowling in the woods.

Neil was sure that strong smell by the bridge was from a big cat, marking its hunting ground. It was like the strong cat smell he'd smelled at the zoo.

He was sure the noises in the wood the other night were from a large animal.

Then there were the claw marks. He knew a big cat on the prowl could kill someone.

"You look totally serious all of a sudden," Tanya said. "You look way better when you smile."

She gave a squeal of laughter and threw her head back.

Neil laughed too as Tanya snorted, with one hand hiding her mouth and the other brushing hair from her eyes.

Their giggles died and an awkward silence fell. But the silence was broken when a large rock flew by them and cracked onto a tree. Tanya screamed.

CHAPTER 4

CRAZY JOE

The echo of the rock hitting the tree hung in the cold air. Crows sprang from the trees and the sky filled with their startled cries. A figure stood on the bank, his breath steaming as he laughed.

"Did I wake you up?" he called.

"You idiot!" Tanya shouted back, her face red with anger.

"Just a joke to keep you on your toes," the guy said. He walked toward them.

It was Joe Linsey, who worked in the kennels.

"What do you think you're doing? You could have hit one of us," Neil shouted.

"Calm down. I know what I'm doing. I was aiming for that tree, and that's just what I hit. Bull's-eye." Joe laughed.

Tanya turned, still angry. "How did you know I was here? Did you follow me?"

"Just keeping my eye on you, Tanya," he said. "After all, the huge beast could be after you."

He turned to Neil. "I see you're having a little talk with my pretty Tanya. Remember me from school?"

Of course Neil remembered him. People at school used to stay away from Joe.

Joe would stand in the corner of the schoolyard and talk the whole time. Some kids called him the Professor. Most kids just said he was crazy.

"How could I forget you?" Neil said. "Still crazy, I see."

Tanya smiled again. "You're right. I don't know what I see in him. I must have a weakness for crazy guys!" She laughed.

Joe looked Neil in the eye. "Have you seen this big cat, the panther on the loose? The woods aren't safe for humans."

Tanya rolled her eyes. "Oh, here he goes. He's going to start a big speech, all about how we are hurting nature."

Joe ignored her. "If you attack one of nature's children, nature will strike back!"

Tanya reached for his hand. "He's crazy, but he's good with the dogs, aren't you?"

"They know I'm in charge." Joe smiled.

Neil couldn't understand what Tanya saw in Joe.

"He lets me sketch the dogs. I'm going to the hunt Saturday, to paint a pheasant," Tanya said, as if she'd read Neil's mind.

Joe snorted. "You'll need to use a lot of red when they rip it apart."

"You could come and join us, Neil," Tanya said. "We meet at the Nelson Inn at eleven o'clock. It's the first hunt of the season."

Joe sneered. "He'll be working. He's got to keep these woods safe from trespassers. It must be hard on his own, without his boss. And lonely. When do you get time off?"

Neil didn't like the questions. Why did Joe care?

High above the treetops across the river, the crows swarmed like angry flies. Joe's eyes scanned the sky. "Ah, there it is," he said. "Our feathered friend."

A large bird rose above the hills, soaring on the air currents. It circled with outstretched wings as the crows flew away.

"You could sketch that vulture, if Neil will let you get close," Joe said to Tanya.

Neil didn't say anything. He knew Joe was testing him.

The bird wasn't a vulture. This bird was smaller, with pointed wing tips. It was a peregrine falcon. Neil loved to watch it wheel above the woods, calling to its mate.

But it was a rare sight. And only Neil knew the exact tree where it nested.

The local pair of falcons brought bird watchers from far and wide. But they brought other people, too, who were looking for ways to make easy money.

Some would pay thousands for eggs, chicks, or even a dead adult to stuff in a glass case. Some hunters were greedy.

He watched Joe's gaze follow the now tiny dot far above them. Neil knew it was time to be on his guard.

Later that evening, Neil knew he was right. Another badger nest had been dug up. It was ripped apart and all the young badgers were gone.

Not far away, one of the pheasant pens was damaged. Feathers lay scattered in the mud. They blew in the evening breeze, across the bloodstained grass.

CHAPTER 5

A MESSAGE
IN BLOOD

Neil had a lot on his mind. He was worried about the strange noises and smells in the woods at night. He was worried about what was killing badgers and pheasants. He was worried about poachers and people who might be after the falcons. He was worried about Joe Linsey.

He wished Jeff was back at work. He'd know what to do. But Neil needed some advice now. He decided to go see Jeff.

A cold wind swept across the field. It was already dark when Neil left work, and a pale moon peeped above the trees.

He knew Jeff would say rain was coming. It was another one of his sayings.

"Pale moon does rain, red moon does blow. White moon does neither rain nor snow."

Sure enough, Jeff mentioned the moon almost as soon as Neil walked in.

"On Friday you'll be able to work all night. It's Hunter's Moon, the brightest moon of the year. She'll be a beauty, too. We're in for a frosty spell after a drop of rain, and a nasty old wind tonight."

Jeff was pale and still in pain. Even so, he wanted to know all about the things Neil had been doing.

"I hope you're ready for the big shoot this weekend. We've got to give them a good time this season. This is our last chance," Jeff said, sounding worried.

Jeff had been having money problems lately. He'd had to sell part of his land.

His face showed the strain as he spoke softly, with a slight tremble in his voice. "You'll take care, won't you, Neil? 'Beware the nights of Hunter's Moon, when all beasts dance to another tune.' It's an old saying around here. But this year it's Halloween, too. Please be careful."

Neil had never heard Jeff talk like that before. There was a different look in his eyes.

Neil felt sorry for his boss as he lay there, looking weak and in pain.

Maybe he shouldn't make Jeff worry about anything else. He clearly had enough on his mind.

But it was Jeff who mentioned the panther. "Have you seen any sign of this big cat on the loose? Everyone's talking about it. I wish I was back on my feet to sort things out."

Jeff sighed. "You need to be on the alert, Neil. My woods have a lot of temptations for a greedy person, like falcons, badgers, and our pheasants. A thief could take everything and get big money. But that's not all."

Before Jeff could finish, a brick smashed through the window. Glass fell like rain around them. The fire roared as an icy blast ripped at the curtains.

Neil rushed to pick up the brick. It was wrapped in paper. The paper was covered with writing.

Neil uncrumpled the paper and read: Beware the dogs. It was scrawled in what looked like blood.

CHAPTER 6

FENBY

A storm later that night snapped thick branches like sticks.

As soon as it was light, Neil headed to the woods to look for damage. There was no wind now. All was deathly quiet.

Neil's heart sank. A fence was down. A fallen tree had smashed one of the tool sheds. Wires were down and power was off in the town. At least the pheasant pens were still in one piece.

The walnut trees at the edge of the woods were still standing. Neil always kept an eye on those. The timber could sell for thousands of dollars. That was another reason they had to guard the woods. Just like that bank robbery in Newport, crime wasn't only in the big cities.

Somewhere behind him a twig snapped. Neil looked around. Nothing stirred. His heart raced. Was the creature behind him? He reached down to pick up a stick. Just then, he saw a shape on the track. His heart missed a beat. The stick rose in his hand.

A black animal ran toward him in a spray of leaves. Neil felt a scream rise in his throat.

A voice rang out through the trees. "Here, boy!"

The labrador wagged its tail and barked playfully. Neil sighed with relief.

"Here, boy. Don't worry, Neil. He's harmless," a man's voice said.

It was Mr. Fenby. He bent down to clip a leash on the dog's collar. "He's excited. He saw something big back there. I'm pretty sure it was the cat. It made me scared, I can tell you. But the dogs will find it for sure."

Mr. Fenby was a good outdoorsman and hunter, especially when it came to pheasant and ducks. He and his wife even kept horses, although town gossip said she'd just left him.

"I hope you're not going to look for that cat now," Neil said. "We need you for the big pheasant hunt coming up."

Mr. Fenby didn't seem to like being told what he couldn't do. "That's a shame. I see there are a few trees down, Neil. A nasty storm, wasn't it?"

Neil looked curiously at the bag in Mr. Fenby's hand.

"Oh, I hope you don't mind," Mr. Fenby said. "I'm just getting some breakfast. Don't worry, I stayed on the public path. I haven't gone into Jeff's private woods. There are lots of mushrooms this year. By the way, how is Jeff these days?"

"Not too good, I'm afraid," Neil said. "Last night, someone threw a brick through his window. There was a note on it, with writing. 'Beware the dogs.' Jeff said it was just a kid playing a prank."

"There are some strange people around, Neil. But if it said dogs — hmmm. I bet Joe knows something about it. He's odd, that guy," Mr. Fenby said. "Well, I better take my mushrooms home. See you, Neil."

Mr. Fenby walked off.

Neil barely noticed. He was too busy thinking. He was sure Joe was behind the vandalism in the woods and the brick through Jeff's window.

Neil gripped his stick. He felt anger rising. Sooner or later, he would have to talk with Joe Linsey face to face.

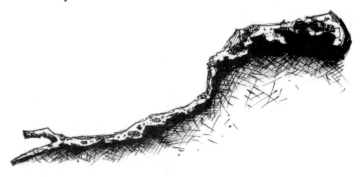

CHAPTER 7

BEWARE THE DOGS

There was a lot of work to be done for the pheasant hunt that weekend. The hunt had to be a success. One more bad season and Jeff might have to sell the rest of his farm. Other people were already trying to buy the land.

The sun spilled into the woods and sparkled in the stream. The bridge lay sprawled on the bank, where it had fallen when Jeff had his accident.

Neil stood by the broken timber.

He felt uneasy. He looked over his shoulder. There was a strange feeling around him. He shivered.

Smashed wood lay on both sides of the stream. But the posts were still firm. Neil looked closer. Two posts weren't splintered like the others. They had cuts, as if someone had cut through the supports on purpose, someone who wanted to hurt Jeff.

Neil was angry. Ahead of him on the path was a sickening sight.

The bright body of a bird lay limp in a pile of leaves. A falcon was dead. It had been shot.

Neil bent and stroked the bird's head. His anger exploded. There was no doubt in his mind: This was Joe's work.

Now it was time to strike back.

Neil stormed into the kennel yard. Dogs yelped and barked. Joe was cleaning out one of the dog pens.

"I need to talk to you, Linsey." Neil waved a stick above his head.

Joe looked up.

"Calm down, dude," he said. "And watch who you're shouting at or I'll jump this wall and show you who's boss around here."

Neil brought the stick down on the wall with a crack.

Blood rose in his cheeks and his eyes flashed with anger.

"First you smash stuff in our woods. Then you saw through the bridge. You tore up badger nests. Now you shot the falcon. You just want to scare us out, don't you? You want to get rid of us so you can get your hands on our woods." Neil was boiling with anger.

Joe jumped over the wall. "Prove it!"

Neil jabbed the stick at Joe's chest. "And you think you can scare Jeff with a brick and a stupid note about Hunter's Moon. You can't deny it."

Joe grabbed Neil's collar. "Listen. I don't know what you're talking about, but I'll give you ten seconds to get off my land."

Neil went on. "Did you write it in the blood of some animal you killed? And what does 'Beware the dogs' mean?"

Joe paused. He let go of Neil's shirt. "Interesting," he said. "Very interesting."

A Land Rover pulled up at the end of the drive.

"Sorry, Neil," Joe said. "I can't give you the punch you deserve. You'll have to wait. Some of us have to plan for the hunt. Let's face it, I'm not some coward who would throw a rock and then run away."

Joe walked off down the driveway. After a few strides, he stopped and looked back at Neil. "Get a clue, Neil. 'Beware the dogs' is from that Halloween saying, the one that kids around here use to scare each other."

Joe reached the Land Rover, jumped inside, and then roared off.

Neil stood and stared after the truck until the smoke cleared.

Neil went to the town library and headed to the folklore section. He picked up a book on Halloween. He looked through the index for the word "dogs."

Then he found it.

"Beware the dogs that prowl the woods

And growl a Halloween tune,

But most of all, beware the cat

That hunts by the Hunter's Moon!"

For a second time that morning a shiver ran down Neil's spine. Tonight was Hunter's Moon. What did it all mean? The clock clunked, twelve hollow clangs: noon. Just twelve hours to go until the Hunter's Moon, a full moon on Halloween night.

CHAPTER 8

TANYA TELLS THE TRUTH

The air was crisp and clear. All afternoon, Neil had been cutting up fallen branches with a chainsaw. Now he was ready to light a bonfire.

Taking a box of matches from his pocket, he bent to light the paper. He paused, remembering the other night when he dropped the whole box.

He was sure he heard a sound behind him, and he looked over his shoulder.

He got to his feet and grabbed the chainsaw. He listened, waiting, as the moon climbed into the sky and the first stars gleamed above him.

Something was moving through the woods, coming nearer. Neil could only see the gray shapes of tree trunks and pheasants.

Suddenly he saw a shadow moving toward him through the stillness: a girl with long dark hair. She was running straight toward him. It was Tanya, gasping for breath.

"I knew you'd be here somewhere," she said, panting. "I'm so glad I found you. I need to talk to you. I've got to tell you something. You can put that chainsaw down now. I'm not the panther!"

Neil smiled. "Come over here while I light the fire."

The flames flared as the bonfire crackled to life. Neil poked the branches, and sparks showered into the night.

"Go on. What do you need to tell me?" he asked.

"It's Joe," Tanya said. "He's really sick. I found him this afternoon. He couldn't stand up. I called the ambulance. He told me to come and tell you, something about Hunter's Moon and walnut trees. It didn't make sense, but he said you'd know. He said you should be warned. He said you need to keep watch tonight."

Neil looked into Tanya's eyes.

She wasn't acting. This was real. She clung on to his arm.

"I don't know what's going on, but it's something scary," Tanya went on.

She paused, then continued, "Joe said he was planning to come up here at midnight to get proof. What did he mean?"

Neil said nothing. He didn't want to tell Tanya that he hated Joe.

But what Tanya said next took his breath away.

"You're probably wondering why I didn't go with him to the hospital," she said. Then she paused. "The thing is, I can't stand him. It's all an act. You could even call me a spy. I'm doing it for the protesters at school."

Neil frowned. What did she mean?

"You know," she went on, "the hunt protesters. We're planning a big thing to disrupt the hunt on Saturday." Tanya sighed.

"I agreed to get some inside information by being nice to Joe," she continued. "I came today to get a few names and addresses of people going to the hunt. It was horrible to find him lying on the floor, but I still hate all he stands for. Animals have a right to live too!"

Neil stared into the flames.

"Then you must hate me, too," he said. "I raise birds for people to hunt. I bet you protestors don't like that, do you?"

Tanya touched his knee. "I don't know. It's complicated. Besides, you seem to respect nature, too."

Neil smiled. "So," he said, "how about joining me here tonight to see what Joe was so worried about?"

"Are you asking me on a date?" Tanya said, smiling.

Neil blushed. "No. Sorry, I mean . . ."

"I'm only teasing," Tanya said. "I think you're right. I think we should hide here tonight and see just what this is all about, to find out the truth, once and for all."

CHAPTER 9

SPIES

Neil and Tanya sat in a coffee shop next to a warm, blazing fireplace.

"Make the most of this heat," Neil said. "It'll be freezing out there tonight."

"I'm wearing extra layers," Tanya said, "and I brought a thermos of coffee for tonight."

She looked over her shoulder and then whispered, "Don't you think we should tell the police?"

Neil sighed. "I reported the dead falcon today, but they can't seem to do much." He shook his head.

Then he went on. "And what do we tell them? That we're camping out tonight because we think something odd is going on? We're looking for a big cat on the prowl? They'd lock us up!"

Tanya sipped her coffee. "Joe's mom called. He's still very sick. They pumped out his stomach and he can't have visitors. They wouldn't say any more."

Neil didn't say anything.

When they left the coffee shop, the moon was already high in the sky.

The whole town was bathed in its cold, silver light.

A sharp frost crept over the trees. A thin crust of ice crawled across the puddles on the trails.

Neil's boots crunched on the ice as they entered the woods.

Even inside the woods, where the trees were thick and tall, the silver light splashed into pools of moonlight. But the shadows grew deeper and darker.

The cloak of night pulled tighter around them. Tanya's hand slipped into Neil's.

"Over there!" Neil pointed with his flashlight beam into a thick mass of bushes. "We can hide in there. We'll be able to see the walnut trees."

Tanya squeezed his hand. "I'm really scared. I have my cell phone ready, just in case."

"Who will you call, Panthers 'R' Us?" Neil joked. His flashlight beam danced over the ground.

"What are you looking for? Tracks?" Tanya asked.

Neil didn't reply. A part of the puzzle fell into place in his mind.

Soon they were sitting, wrapped in their sleeping bags. Their eyes watched the ghostly woods. Their flashlights were off.

It was almost midnight and an icy silence hung in the cold darkness.

Enough moonlight seeped across the ground so they could see smudgy shapes. But they heard it first.

A scraping noise, the rustle of leaves and the cracking of dry twigs.

Panting. Something being dragged. Grunting.

Neil gripped Tanya's arm as a figure came closer. Or were there two shapes? It was hard to see. There was a thud.

The shape moved away again. Silence. Tanya squeezed Neil's hand. They waited.

A shrill sound startled them. It was Tanya's watch beeping. She covered her wrist and the noise died.

The moon was high overhead now. Its milky light soaked into the earth around them. It seeped through the walnut trees and onto the advancing figure.

The figure of a man, carrying something. Neil's eyes were fixed on the man, who was scraping a tool on tree trunks.

Tanya could wait no longer. She had to ask Neil what was going on.

But it wasn't just Neil's grip on her arm that stopped her. It was the footsteps, coming nearer, very close.

Liquid splashed around them. The smell made their eyes water.

Neil felt drips fall on his hand. He looked down. It shone in the moonlight.

He felt sick.

His hand was covered in blood.

He thought of the words he'd read earlier.

"But most of all, beware the cat

That hunts by the Hunter's Moon!"

CHAPTER 10

THE DIGGING SHADOW

The man began to dig. The moon shone more brightly than ever. His shovel gleamed like silver. The frozen earth crunched with each blow of the shovel.

"Can you see who he is?" Neil asked, but he had a good idea already. It was all starting to make sense. He'd have to find out if he was right. He stood up.

"I'm going down there," he said. "Watch, but stay out of sight." He slowly crept from tree to tree.

The man stopped digging every so often to look around. Neil stayed in the shadows just a few yards away.

The hole in the ground was the size of a grave. Neil stepped forward, his heart thumping like crazy.

He was about to speak when the man turned and jumped at Neil with the spade.

Neil fell with a blinding crack as the shovel struck his shoulder. The man lifted the shovel above his head like an ax. He was about to bring it down with a terrible crash.

Then something hit the man hard. He staggered and fell, sinking into the soft pile of earth.

When Neil sat up, he realized that Tanya had thrown a large rock at the man.

As the shadowy figure lay on the ground, the man howled. Like a beast, like a hunted tiger, bathed by the light of Hunter's Moon.

CHAPTER 11

WHAT HAPPENED
TO FENBY?

It was the day of the hunt. Jeff had told Neil to forget about going to work that day. Neil needed rest, and besides, the police would be searching the woods.

The morning mist drifted across the valley. Jeff looked out his window and sighed. A dead cow lay in the field. Its throat had been torn, and there were deep claw marks across its back.

Jeff turned to Neil and Tanya.

"It happened last night," he said. "No panther, just your friend with his iron claw. At least you stopped him."

He rubbed his back. It was already much better. "I'll make some coffee."

"I'll do it," Tanya said as she jumped to her feet.

Neil was still dazed from lack of sleep and the blow to his shoulder. He had to get stitches and was wearing a sling on his arm. Then there had been all the police questions. He'd only slept for an hour or so.

Jeff sighed. "You only gave him a scare and a big bruise, not enough to stop him from running off. Let's hope the police have picked him up by now."

"Yeah. Tanya saved me by throwing that rock," Neil said.

Then he told Joe the whole story of Fenby, the man with the dark secret, the one who tried to stop them from finding out the truth.

"Fenby was one of the robbers who held up that bank in Newport," explained Neil. "He was looking for a place to bury the cash, until things cooled off and the police stopped looking for it. So where did he plan to hide it? The woods. How did he make sure people didn't go snooping around and find out what he was up to? He made up the panther story. He used an iron claw to scratch the trees. He splashed blood around. He threw that brick through your window. He wrecked the bridge to get you out of the way."

Neil took a deep breath. "He spilled ammonia, which smelled horrible," he went on. "It was to keep dogs from digging up his loot."

"And do you know why he waited until Hunter's Moon to bury it?" Jeff asked. "It's the only night of the year when it's light enough to see in those woods without a flashlight. A flashlight would be seen by anyone walking past the woods. Fenby couldn't take the risk of being caught."

"Joe figured out what was going on," Tanya said, walking back into the room. "That's why Fenby asked him over for a meal, to poison him."

Neil lay down on the sofa. "Poison from our own woods. Fenby picked poison mushrooms, then invited Joe over to dinner. They could have killed him."

The phone rang and Jeff went into the hall.

Neil took Tanya's hand.

"Thanks for everything," he said. "You not only saved my life last night, you saved our woods. That greedy Fenby wanted Jeff's land. He was waiting for us to fail this season. Then he was going to buy the land with his stolen money from the bank. But we're not going to fail now. Plus we got the reward for turning him in to the police."

Tanya smiled. "I'm going to cook a feast for us tonight. For you, Jeff, and me."

Neil laughed. "No mushrooms, I hope!" he said, smiling. He turned as Jeff came back in the room.

Jeff looked pale.

"That was my son," Jeff said. "He comes every night to check on my cows. He was held up last night. He didn't get here till midnight."

"He said all the cows were fine," Jeff went on. "That can only mean one thing: Fenby wasn't the one who killed that cow. There's something else out there."

Tanya looked at Neil.

"But do you want to hear something even stranger?" Jeff asked. "My son saw an ambulance and police cars this morning on his side of the woods. Someone found Fenby in a ditch. It looked like he'd been attacked by something."

Neil stood and walked to the window. A soft wind stirred the trees. A single falcon flew high above the woods. It was a peaceful scene.

But there were still secrets out there, dark secrets, known only to the night and the silent Hunter's Moon.

ABOUT THE AUTHOR

John Townsend has been in teaching for 25 years, and has been a full-time writer since January 2003. He has written more than sixty books for young people, on such wide-ranging subjects as monsters, urban legends, spiders, computer crime, and spies. He has also written the recent thrillers *The Hand* and *The Omen and the Ghost*. He lives in England.

ABOUT THE ILLUSTRATOR

Sean Dietrich was born in Baltimore, Maryland and now lives in San Diego, California. He's been drawing since the age of 4. He had his first art show at age 6, self published his first comic book at 16, and has won more than 53 art awards throughout the years. When he's not drawing, Dietrich says he spends too much time in front of the tv playing video games.

GLOSSARY

ammonia (uh-MOH-nyuh)—a strong liquid that is sometimes used for cleaning

badger (BAD-jur)—a small mammal with sharp claws that lives in an underground burrow or nest

dappled (DAP-uhld)—covered in spots and patches of light. Sunlight shining through a tree's leaves will make the ground below look dappled.

lurked (LURKT)—to hide, ready for an attack

peregrine falcon (PAIR-uh-grin FALL-kun)— a large hunting bird that catches other birds for food

pheasant (FEZ-uhnt)—a bird that is popular with hunters

screeched (SKREECHT)—screamed or squeaked loudly

spine (SPYN)—the backbone

weasel (WEE-zuhl)—a small, slender mammal with sharp teeth and soft fur

DISCUSSION QUESTIONS

1. Why did Neil suspect Joe of killing the birds? Was there a reason the two young men didn't like each other?

2. Do you think it is all right for people to raise animals that will be hunted? How is that different than raising animals to be eaten for food? Explain your answers.

3. When Neil reads about the Hunter's Moon and the Halloween legend, do you think he believes it? Do you know of any legends or tales that people like to tell to scare each other?

WRITING PROMPTS

1. Imagine you are in the woods, camping out with friends, telling scary stories. What is a scary story that you could make up to frighten your friends?

2. Tanya and Neil stay in the woods at night to try to solve the mystery of the panther. What would happen if they saw a real panther? What would they do? How would they escape from the creature?

3. Jeff, Neil's boss and friend, knows a lot about nature and plants and animals. Is there an animal, or pet, or part of nature that you know a lot about? Write down what you know.

MORE
SHADE BOOKS!

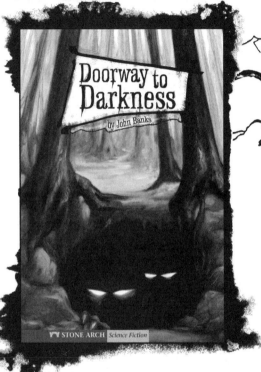

Doorway to
Darkness
by John Banks

STONE ARCH Science Fiction

Luke and Lisa are protesting with a group of friends at a construction site. They don't want the new road cutting through old Mott Hill. Suddenly, one of the diggers disappears into the ground! Have the workers stumbled on an opening to another world?

Sammi and Jak are thrilled when Chad takes them on a trip to explore a new planet. Then disaster strikes and they are stranded, surrounded by deadly spear plants! If only they could get back to their ship.

INTERNET SITES

Do you want to know more about subjects related to this book? Or are you interested in learning about other topics? Then check out FactHound, a fun, easy way to find Internet sites.

Our investigative staff has already sniffed out great sites for you!

Here's how to use FactHound:

1. Visit *www.facthound.com*

2. Select your grade level.

3. To learn more about subjects related to this book, type in the book's ISBN number: **1598893521**.

4. Click the **Fetch It** button.

FactHound will fetch the best Internet sites for you!